MOST VALUABLE PLAYERS

MVP

4

THE
BASKETBALL BLOWOUT

MVP

Also by David A. Kelly

The Ballpark Mysteries® series

MOST VALUABLE PLAYERS

MVP

4

THE
BASKETBALL BLOWOUT

David A. Kelly

illustrated by Scott Brundage

A STEPPING STONE BOOK™

Random House 🏠 New York

This book is dedicated to my mother, Nancy Kelly,
who tried to make me a basketball star by bringing
me to the school gym on Saturdays, even though all
I really wanted was to stay home and read.
—D.A.K.

Text copyright © 2017 by David A. Kelly
Cover art and interior illustrations copyright © 2017 by Scott Brundage

All rights reserved. Published in the United States by Random House Children's Books,
a division of Penguin Random House LLC, New York.
Random House and the colophon are registered trademarks and A Stepping Stone Book
and the colophon are trademarks of Penguin Random House LLC.
Ballpark Mysteries® is a registered trademark of Upside Research, Inc.

Visit us on the Web!
SteppingStonesBooks.com
randomhousekids.com

Educators and librarians, for a variety of teaching tools, visit us at RHTeachersLibrarians.com

Library of Congress Cataloging-in-Publication Data is available on request.

ISBN 978-0-553-51328-8 (trade) — ISBN 978-0-553-51329-5 (lib. bdg.) —
ISBN 978-0-553-51330-1 (ebook)

Printed in the United States of America
10 9 8 7 6 5 4 3 2 1

This book has been officially leveled by using the F&P Text Level Gradient™ Leveling System.

CONTENTS

MVP Stats

Meet the MVPs!

MAX

Great athlete—
and a great detective

ALICE

Archery ace
and animal lover

NICO

Can't wait to practice
and can't wait to play

LUKE

Loves to exercise
his funny bone

KAT

Captures the best
game-day moment
on camera

The Runaway

The basketball flew through the air toward the net. It bounced on the orange hoop, tottered for a moment, and then fell backward.

No basket!

"Oh no!" Luke moaned. It was Monday after school. He and four friends were in the Franklin Elementary School gym, practicing for their weekend travel tournament.

Luke's buddy Nico stepped up to the free throw line. He lofted a ball toward the basket. *Whoosh!* It dropped perfectly through the net. One point!

"Yahoo! Six for six!" Nico called out. "You only made one shot so far, Luke. You've got some catching up to do!"

"Oh yeah?" Luke said. "Watch this!" He grabbed Nico's rebound and ran to the free throw line as he dribbled the ball. He stopped and turned around so he had his back to the basket. Luke loved trying trick shots more than he liked practicing.

He tilted his head way back and looked for the basket. It was upside down. Luke lobbed the ball over his head! Then he turned to watch.

"Not again!" he cried. The ball hit the top corner of the backboard. Then it bounced off the wall of the gym. Luke's twin sister, Kat, scrambled over to pick up the ball as it rolled away.

Nico laughed and nodded. "It's going to take more than a trick shot to beat me," he said. Nico was the school's best athlete. He once made twenty-five free throws in a row! "You're going to have to work on the basics if we'll have a chance at the travel tournament this weekend."

Luke, Nico, Kat, and their two friends Max and Alice called themselves the Most Valuable Players Club. They had all gotten MVP medals for figuring out who was trying to ruin Franklin's school Olympics.

The MVP Club had been practicing

basketball as the blue team for about a month. They even had special blue T-shirts for games. The first basketball travel tournament was that weekend, and the school was sending one team. If their team won a play-off game on Wednesday, the five friends would be going to the tournament. But first they'd have to beat Jenna Lewis and her red team.

For the next ten minutes, Alice, Max, Kat, Luke, and Nico took turns shooting free throws, until it was time for one of the other teams to practice. The red, orange, gold, and purple Franklin basketball teams were all in the gym practicing. Teams not on the court sat in the bleachers, waiting their turns.

TWEET! A whistle pierced the sound of bouncing basketballs. It was Ms. Suraci, the school's PE teacher and basketball coach. She walked into the gym carrying a clipboard and a backpack.

The MVP Club and all the other teams gathered around her. Ms. Suraci blew her whistle again and waved her clipboard in the air for quiet.

"We've got a busy basketball season this year," she said. "Our first travel tournament is this weekend. It's the Big City Basketball Blowout. The play-off game on Wednesday will decide whether the red team or the blue team goes this weekend. But we have lots of other tournaments scheduled, so all the teams will get to travel."

The kids clapped. A chant of *"Red team! Red team! Red team!"* rose up from Jenna and the members of her team. Ms. Suraci waved the clipboard for quiet again.

"Listen, no one will be going anywhere unless we can raise some extra money for travel expenses," she said. Ms. Suraci leaned over and reached into her backpack. "And here's how we're going to do it."

She held up a shiny bag of popcorn. "We're having a fund-raiser for our travel teams," she said. "The school's parent

group has donated all this popcorn. You each need to sell as much popcorn as you can by the end of the week in order to have enough money for this year's tournaments."

Ms. Suraci opened a couple of bags of popcorn and passed them around. Everyone grabbed a few bites and chomped away.

"Mmm...this is good," Kat whispered to Alice. "I'll take some more!"

"What do we get if we sell the popcorn?" Tim Reagan on the gold team asked.

"Good question," Ms. Suraci replied. "You get to play travel basketball!"

Everyone laughed.

Ms. Suraci rustled around in her backpack. "But we do have prizes, based on how much each team sells," she said. "The team that sells the second-most popcorn wins five of these." She held up a bright-green T-shirt. It had pictures of popcorn all over it.

"Wow!" said some of the kids.

"Neat," Max whispered to Alice.

"But the team that sells the *most* popcorn wins these!" Ms. Suraci said. She held up a bright-green sweatshirt that read *FRANKLIN BASKETBALL.*

"I want that," Luke said.

"But that's not all," Ms. Suraci said. "The *person* on the winning team who sells the most popcorn gets the grand prize!" She reached into the backpack and lifted up the coolest pair of sneakers the kids had ever seen. They had special black-and-silver soles, with red stripes running up the sides.

"Oh man, that's great!" Peter Paterson from the purple team said. "Those look *fast!*"

"Hey, those are the brand-new ones that just came out," a boy named Nolan said.

"The winner of the contest will get a pair in his or her size," Ms. Suraci said. "Tom's Sneaker Store on Main Street is donating them. I wish we had enough for a whole team, but we don't. If you want to win the sneakers, your *team* has to sell the most popcorn compared to other teams, and *you* have to sell the most popcorn on your team."

The kids rushed forward to inspect the sneakers and shirts. Max held up a T-shirt. "That would look great on you," Kat said. Nico picked up a sneaker. It felt super light in his hands.

TWEET! Ms. Suraci blew her whistle again. "Follow me!" she called. She led everyone to her office. Ms. Suraci had a huge pile of popcorn bags in the corner.

"Everyone starts with thirty," she said. "But if you need more, stop in and see me."

Ms. Suraci handed out the larger bags full of single-serving popcorn packages. Each team stepped forward to get their popcorn, then ran outside to start selling it. The MVP Club's blue team was last.

As soon as they got their popcorn,

Max and Alice headed for the door.

"Hang on," Nico called. "Not so fast!"

The MVP Club looked at Nico.

"Why not?" Alice asked. "We've got to start selling."

Nico waved his hand in the direction of the gym at the end of the hallway. "We *will,* but first we should practice for half an hour," he said. "After all, now we've got the gym to ourselves! And we need more practice before Wednesday's game if we're going to win." A big empty gym was one of Nico's favorite places to be in the whole world.

"Ugh!" Luke groaned. "Practice, shmactice! Everyone is out selling popcorn, and we're not!"

"Yes, but we'll be the ones winning the game on Wednesday and heading to the Big City Basketball Blowout this weekend!" Nico said. "It will be worth it. We'll still have time to sell popcorn later. Come on!"

Nico led the MVP Club back down

the hall to the gym. But as they got closer, they could hear that the gym wasn't empty! Someone was shooting baskets.

"Hey, who's that?" Nico said. "Someone else is practicing! I thought everyone was gone!"

Nico ran to the doors of the gym and pulled them open. The MVP Club burst inside.

On the far side of the gym, there was a boy shooting baskets.

"Hey, what are you doing here?" Max called out.

The boy grabbed the ball and swung around. He stared at the members of the MVP Club for a moment.

Then he dropped the ball and took off running!

Popcorn Challenge

"Hey!" Max said. "Stop him!"

The MVP Club raced after the boy. But he ran toward a door at the far end of the gym and disappeared. The door slammed shut.

"Quick, he went outside!" Alice said.

The MVP Club skidded to a halt. Alice was about to grab the door handle when Nico stopped her.

"Hang on," Nico said. "We can just wait here."

"Are you kidding?" Alice asked. "Why don't we chase him?"

Nico smiled. "Because we don't have to!" he said. He took a step back and pointed to a door farther down the wall. *"That's* the door that goes outside," he said. *"This* one just goes to the supply closet! There's only once place he can go, and it's back out here!"

The rest of the MVP Club looked at the door. Then Luke laughed. "That's great!" he said. He plopped down cross-legged on the ground. "This is my kind of chase. One where we can just sit and wait."

While Luke relaxed, Nico moved closer to the door. He knocked on it. "Hey, come on out!" he called. "We didn't mean to scare you. We just didn't think anyone else would be in the gym!"

"Hey, Nico!" Luke said. "No need to rush things to get back to our practice!" He pulled out one of his bags of popcorn, ripped it open, and poured some into his hand. "And look! I've already made my first sale. I'm one step ahead of you in winning those sneakers!" he said. "Get it! One step?"

Max groaned. "That's bad," he said. "And that will be a pretty expensive pair of sneakers if you try to win them by buying all the popcorn yourself!"

Luke smiled and rubbed his tummy. "At least I wouldn't be hungry!" he said. He laughed again and stuffed another handful of popcorn in his mouth. But the popcorn went down the wrong way. He let out a big cough and pieces of fluffy, wet popcorn fell all over the gym floor.

Kat rolled her eyes as Luke tried to scoop up the kernels. "But you'll still be messy," Kat said. "Just like you are at home!"

Suddenly, the door to the supply closet cracked open. A pair of brown eyes peeked out from behind the edge of the door.

"Come on out," Nico said. "We're not going to bite!" He stepped forward and pulled the door all the way open.

Behind it stood a short, thin boy.

"Hey, you're in my class. You're Jason, right?" Max asked. "You just started a few weeks ago."

The boy's brown curly hair bounced as he nodded. "Yeah," he said softly. Jason was wearing a colorful shirt with a picture of a soccer player on it. His jeans looked a bit scruffy, and his shoelaces were broken.

Nico stepped forward. "I'm Nico," he said. He pointed at the other members of the MVP Club. "That's Alice, Kat, and Luke. I guess you know Max because he's in your class. Why did you run?"

The boy shrugged. "I wasn't sure I was allowed to be here," he said. "I didn't want to get in any trouble."

"I'm sure Ms. Suraci wouldn't mind. Why don't you come shoot hoops with us?" Nico asked. "We have to practice for our game on Wednesday."

The MVP Club and Jason followed

Nico to the hoop near the door of the gym. They each took turns taking ten shots. As usual, Nico came in first with seven baskets. Alice got five. Max, Luke, and Jason tied with four. Kat made three.

Jason checked the time. "That was fun, but I have to get going," he said.

"You're not bad," Nico said. "Why didn't you join a basketball team?"

"I can't," Jason said. "I have stuff that I have to do in the afternoon. But thanks for letting me practice. See you tomorrow!"

After Jason left, Nico made the MVP Club practice for another twenty minutes. When they were finally done, Nico put the basketball back in the corner and then ran to the group. But just before he reached them, Nico threw his hands up in the air, leaned over, and did two back handsprings! He took

gymnastics on the weekends and had more bounce in him than most people. He landed right in front of the group and flexed his muscles for fun.

"Seven out of ten shots. Not bad, eh?" he said. "I guess my basketball muscles are strong today."

"Maybe they are," said Luke. "But it's not your basketball muscles that matter now. It's your popcorn muscles. And I'll bet they're not as strong as mine!"

Nico dropped his arms and stood tall. "Oh yeah?" he asked. "There's no way I'm losing that challenge." Nico stuck out his leg and moved his foot around. "You won't have to wait too long to see those cool sneakers on *my* feet!"

Luke shook his head. "I've got a secret plan," he said. "And you won't be able to beat me."

Ghost Dogs

"So what's your secret plan?" Alice asked Luke. It was Tuesday morning and Alice, Luke, and Kat had just locked their bikes in the racks and were walking toward the school.

"Um," Luke said. "It's a plan for beating Nico."

Alice nodded. "I know that," she said. "But how are you going to sell more popcorn?"

Luke glanced at Alice. Then he looked over to the playground and pointed. "Hey, they put a new swing on the swing set," he said. "We should go check it out during recess."

Kat sighed. "Stop trying to change the subject!" she said. Kat nudged Luke. "Like I told you last night, you don't have a chance. If there's a competition to win, Nico won't quit. If there's something that requires work, like selling popcorn, you won't start! Come on, Luke! You know you'd rather just hang out and read your comic books than sell popcorn."

Luke stopped. "Kat, stay out of this!" he said. "I do have a plan. I just don't want to tell anyone. I don't want anyone stealing my secret."

"Oh yeah, your secret," Kat said. She smiled at Alice and shook her head. "The only thing he's done is sell one bag of popcorn to our parents and one to our grandmother. But they bought bags from me, too, so he's no closer to winning those sneakers than I am."

"Well, you both need to get moving," Alice said. She opened her backpack and took out a list. "I sold six bags of popcorn last night. Two to my family and four to our neighbors. I'm going out this afternoon to sell more. Looks like I might be the one lacing up those sneakers next week!"

The kids ran up the steps to school. It was just a few minutes before the first bell, so the hallways were crowded. A clump of students was standing across from the main office. They were studying something on the wall.

It was a huge poster that listed everyone's name and how many bags of popcorn they'd sold. Ms. Suraci must have put it up that morning. The sign next to it said to report all sales to Ms. Suraci and she would post the numbers each day.

Luke dropped his backpack. "Aww,

why do they have to do this?" he asked. "They should just let us add everything up at the end of the week!"

Kat snickered. "Luke, maybe this was Ms. Suraci's secret plan," she said. "Her secret plan to get everyone to go out and sell more popcorn!"

BRIIIIIIIING!

The school bell rang. The kids scrambled to get to their homerooms before they were late.

BRIIIIIIIING!

The last bell rang for the day. The kids of Franklin Elementary flooded into the hallways and ran for the doors.

The members of the MVP Club gathered on the front steps of the school.

"Did you come up with a real plan yet, Luke?" Nico teased. "Or are you going to eat your way to victory?"

Luke stopped and turned to face

Nico. "You'll just have to wait and see," he said. "You might be able to win at basketball, but I'm going to win those sneakers!"

Nico backed up a step. "Oh, okay," he said. "You can try to win them, but I think you'll see those sneakers on *my* feet on Friday. I sold six bags last night."

"Guys, why don't you work together?" Alice asked. "Neither of you will win the sneakers unless *our team* sells the most popcorn!"

Luke and Nico both shook their heads. "No way!" Luke said. "We're going to see which one of us is better!"

"Okay," Alice said. "If that's what you want."

The group continued walking in silence until they were about halfway home. "Hey, look at that!" Alice said, pointing across the street. "Let's go check it out!"

Jason, the boy from the gym, was walking down the sidewalk. But he wasn't alone. He had three big dogs on leashes!

Alice waited for the light to turn green and then crossed the street. The rest of the MVP Club followed her.

"Hi, Jason," Alice said. "Can I pet your dogs?"

"Sure. They'd like that." Jason smiled. "This is Sammy, Dexter, and Cupcake."

Alice dropped down in front of the three dogs and started petting them. They rushed forward and gave her slobbering kisses with their tongues. Alice smiled from ear to ear. Even though she had three dogs of her own at home, Alice always loved to meet new ones.

"Hey, Jason, I didn't know you had three dogs just like Alice," Nico said.

"I don't," Jason said. "I actually don't have any."

"Then what are these?" Luke asked. "Ghost dogs?"

Jason laughed. "No, they're real dogs." He reached down and petted Dexter's black fur. "But they're not mine. I just started a dog-walking service. I walk these three every day after school. That's why I can't play basketball." Jason reached into his pocket and pulled out a note card with a phone number on it and a picture of a dog. He handed it to Alice.

"Wow, that's a great idea," Max said. He had always wanted to start a business.

Jason blushed. "Yeah, I thought so," he said. "My mom lost her job recently, so I'm helping out by earning money. I'm trying to find more dogs to walk, but it's hard to get new customers."

Alice stood up. "Maybe we can help," she said. "We can keep our ears open and let you know if we hear of anyone who wants a dog walker. I'll give them your phone number."

"That would be great," Jason said as Dexter jumped up and gave Alice another big kiss. Alice hugged him back.

Jason gave Dexter a tug. "Sorry, but

it's getting late," he said. "I have to drop these guys off and get home."

"Where do you live?" Max asked.

Jason looked down. He scuffed the concrete with his worn sneaker. "Um, I just have to get the dogs back. My mom wanted me to help her with something," he said.

Max looked at Nico and Alice. He raised an eyebrow.

Jason pulled on the leashes. "Come on, boys," he said. He led the dogs down the street. "See you later!" he said.

"Okay, bye!" Max said.

As soon as Jason was out of earshot, Max whispered, "That was weird. He didn't want to tell us where he lived."

The rest of the MVP Club nodded. When Jason was about a block away, Max leaned in. "I've got an idea," he said. "I'm going to investigate. Wait here for me."

Popcorn Problems

"Now what?" Luke asked. "We're never going to get to sell our popcorn!"

Nico turned a cartwheel. "We can wait a few minutes for him," he said. "Let's see what he discovers."

Max crossed the street and followed Jason, but he took care to stay out of sight. Max loved playing detective. His father was chief of police, and Max wanted to be just like him. A minute later, Jason and Max had disappeared around a corner.

Alice and Kat sat cross-legged on

the grass. They opened their backpacks and pulled out books to read. Luke lay on his back and made funny noises with his mouth. Nico practiced walking on his hands.

A short time later, they heard someone running toward them. It was Max!

"So, did you find anything out?" Kat asked.

"Yes!" Max said as he caught his breath. "Jason doesn't live in a house!"

"What do you mean?" Nico asked. "Does he live in a tree?"

"No," Max said. "He lives near the grocery store downtown, in that family shelter building!"

Luke looked up. "He lives in a shed?" he asked. "That's cool! If I lived in the shed in our backyard, maybe my mom wouldn't pester me to clean it up!"

Max rolled his eyes. "No, Luke," he said. "He and his mom live in a *shelter*. It's an apartment building where families can live for a while if they've lost their home."

"No wonder he was trying to earn money after school," Kat said.

Alice and Nico nodded.

"Last year in Sunday school class, we talked about people who lose their homes," Nico said. "Our teacher said that any type of family can end up without a place to live. Sometimes it's just bad luck."

"Maybe we could find a way to help him," Max said.

"Like how?" Luke asked. "Build him a house? I don't think so."

"No," Max said. "We can at least be friendly to him. He's in my class. I can ask him tomorrow if he wants to help our team when he has time. He could take notes on our plays. He can be our sixth man!"

"What's a sixth man?" Alice asked.

"It's the name for a basketball team's extra player," Max said. "Someone who doesn't start in the game but is available to play when needed."

Kat nodded. "I like it!"

"Good idea," Nico said.

Luke nudged Nico. "Well, having Jason as our sixth man will be good, but we've got to earn some money for our team," he said. "And for my feet! They can't wait to try out those new sneakers!"

Nico dropped his hands to the sidewalk and popped his feet up in the air.

"Not so fast! Take a good look at these feet," Nico said as he waggled his upside-down feet in Luke's face. "Because I'm the one who's going to win those sneakers!"

Luke swatted Nico's feet with his hand. Nico wavered back and forth for a moment and then toppled over.

"I'd love to stay and look at your old

sneakers," Luke said. "But my customers are getting hungry for popcorn. Wait until you see my totals tomorrow morning!"

With that, Luke left. Nico popped up and brushed himself off. "Well, I have to go sell popcorn, too," he said. "See you tomorrow morning!"

The MVP Club split up. They agreed to meet at the popcorn poster in school the next morning to see how they did.

Alice and Kat went together to sell popcorn. They started with the houses on Kat's street and worked their way to Alice's house. As soon as someone opened their door, either Alice or Kat would explain why they were selling the popcorn and ask for money. After twenty houses, they had sold eight bags.

Around the corner, Nico set off on his own. He walked to Main Street and went store to store, asking the shopkeepers if

they'd be willing to buy a bag of popcorn to support the basketball teams. After fifteen stores, Nico had sold nine bags of popcorn.

Max took all his popcorn and went to visit his father at the police station. He sat at his father's desk and tried to sell popcorn to all the police officers who came by. After an hour, Max had sold another twelve bags of popcorn.

Luke went to the front of the movie theater. He poured a couple bags of popcorn into a bowl he had brought. He offered a taste of the popcorn to the people heading into the movie theater. They all tried some, and some bought a bag. He had to refill his bowl a few times. When the movie started, Luke had gone through a lot of popcorn.

Luke packed up his bowl and the rest of the popcorn and ran home to count his money.

His mother was cooking dinner when he arrived. Luke plopped his popcorn on the table and counted it. He had used up fourteen bags of popcorn.

"How'd you do?" his mother asked.

"Tell you in a minute," he said.

Luke pulled his money out of his pocket and counted it.

"Oh no!" he said. "I only sold five! I used up nine bags of popcorn as samples. I'm going to have to pay for those myself!"

He flipped the bills through his hand.

"That means I spent almost twice as much buying popcorn for samples as I made selling it," he said. "I would have saved money if I had just stayed home and eaten popcorn all afternoon!"

Team Failure

"How many did you sell?" Nico asked Alice at lunch the next day.

"Fifteen bags!" Alice said. "How about you?"

"Only sixteen," Nico said.

"I sold twelve," Max said. "And my dad's going to bring some more to work today. What about you, Luke?"

Luke pretended not to hear. Kat nudged him. "Luke! Wake up!" she said. "Max asked how many bags you sold. Tell him how your plan worked out."

Luke sighed. "Fourteen," he said.

"That's great!" Alice said.

Kat laughed. "Not quite," she said. "That's how many bags he used up trying to sell popcorn in front of the theater. But how many of those fourteen did you actually sell, Luke?"

Luke shrugged. "Five."

Alice and Max groaned.

"You mean you gave away nine bags of samples?" Nico said. "Oh, that's bad! Let's hope your basketball game is better than your popcorn game!"

Kat tugged on Luke's shirt. "Come on," she said. "Ms. Suraci said today's totals would be up after lunch. Let's go see how all the other teams did."

The MVP Club ran through the school to the poster. A bunch of the other basketball players were already gathered around, checking their totals. When the members of the MVP Club saw the poster, they all went quiet.

Jenna and the red team were winning.

Kat ran her finger down the numbers for Jenna's team. "Twenty-one, seventeen, twenty-five! Fifteen, twenty," she read. "Wow, that's really good!"

Nico and the others nodded. "I thought we were doing well, but I'm not even going to have a chance to win those shirts if this keeps up!" he said.

"I may not even be close to winning those shirts," Luke said. "But all I have to do is go sell seven more, and I'll be ahead of Nico!"

Nico spun around. "Sorry!" he said. "I'm the leader today, and I'll be the leader tomorrow." He held up his foot. "Those new sneakers are going to feel pretty good on my feet on Friday!"

Luke batted Nico's foot away. "You might want to buy some new socks," he said. "Because that's all you'll be wearing on Friday."

Luke hitched up his backpack and walked away.

Alice raised her hand to give a high five. *"Okay,* way to go team!" she said. "I think that means we're going to have a great game today!"

Nico gave a small huff. Kat shrugged and walked to her classroom. Nico and Alice took one last look at the totals poster and headed to class. The MVP Club had a lot of work to do.

The game that afternoon didn't start off much better than that morning's conversation had ended. Luke was still bothered that he didn't sell as much as Nico. Alice, Kat, and Max felt like their team was in trouble. Everyone seemed focused on their own sales numbers and was eager to get out to sell popcorn. They were waiting for Nico inside the gym.

Luke dropped his backpack and slumped down to the floor. "We're not going to have a chance against her in sales *or* the game!" he said. Jenna and the red team were already in the gym practicing. "And that means we won't go to the Big City Basketball Blowout!"

The doors swung open and Nico walked in. "Hey, look who I found on my way here. Our sixth man!" he said. Jason was right behind him. "He said that Max asked him to help us out today."

Jason gave the others a big smile. "I can take notes on your plays and give you feedback," he said. "But I can only do it until halftime because I have to leave to walk the dogs."

"They were *soooo* cute," Alice said. "Maybe I can help you sometime!"

"Sure," Jason said.

Nico clapped his hands. "Let's practice!" The MVP Club pulled their special blue T-shirts over their heads and practiced for fifteen minutes. Nico tried to have them work on passing and dribbling, but everyone kept dropping the ball or missing layups.

TWEET! Ms. Suraci blew her whistle. It was time for the game!

Jason stayed on the side of the gym with a clipboard and a pad of paper.

From the start, it seemed like Jenna's red team was in control. They scored three times in a row. The MVP Club was unable to play together as a team. Every time Nico or Max got the ball, they tried to score, even if someone else with a better shot was open. On the sidelines, Jason kept taking notes and trying to give the MVP Club advice, but no one was listening. By the end of the first quarter, the red team was ahead 12–4. Only Nico and Alice had scored for the blue team.

The MVP Club got off to a good start when the whistle blew for the start of the second quarter. Max passed the ball to Alice. She dribbled down to half-

court. When a red team player got in her way, Alice turned and passed to Luke, who was in the corner and wide open. Luke dribbled toward the basket, leapt up, and shot the ball. It bounced off the backboard and dropped to the rim. The ball spun around the edge of the rim, around and around, but then dropped off! No basket!

The players nearby rushed in for the rebound, but Luke was able to grab it. He was about to try for a shot when Becky from the red team popped up in front of him. Luke swerved to the left. Becky blocked him there, too. But then Luke veered to the right and snuck by. The basket was wide open! Luke dribbled closer and took the open shot. The ball arced to the basket. It landed on the back of the rim and bounced out of bounds.

TWEET! It was the red team's ball. Becky threw it in from the sideline to her teammate Dan. He passed to Jenna, who dribbled the ball down the court. Nico got in front of her, his hands up high to block her view. Jenna sprang to the side and snapped a pass back to Dan. He dribbled hard and raced to the basket. He hooked the ball up. It floated over the rim and dropped into the basket. Another two points for the red team!

The MVP Club didn't score the next

time they got the ball because Luke accidentally tipped the ball out of bounds again. Over on the sidelines, Jason made a note on the clipboard.

When the red team took the ball, Dan passed it to Jenna. The center was wide open, so Jenna dribbled hard toward the basket. Luke spotted her but was too late to stop her. Instead, he reached out and grabbed Jenna's arm as she jumped up to shoot.

TWEET!

"Personal foul! Holding. Blue team," Ms. Suraci called. "Two free throws for the red team."

Jenna took the ball to the foul line while each team lined up near the basket. Jenna studied the basket and then took her shot.

SWISH! She scored!

Ms. Suraci threw the ball back to Jenna. Jenna bounced the ball twice and got ready to take her second free throw.

The players on each team got ready to rebound.

Jenna took her shot. The ball arced toward the basket. But it was high! The basketball hit the edge of the rim and bounced. Then it fell back down toward the court. A cluster of hands from both teams stretched up to grab the ball.

After a moment of fumbling, Nico pulled it away. He spun and dribbled down the court. The MVP Club had a chance to get some points back.

But when Nico went for his shot, his front leg pushed off wrong. He had to twist to keep from falling over, and the ball sailed under the backboard and out of bounds!

Things were not looking good for the MVP Club.

The next few minutes passed quickly, but neither team scored. The MVP Club was still behind by eight points, but the energy seemed to be turning. It was possible they might catch up. With only seconds left in the first half, the blue team ran down the court. Nico dribbled expertly around two defenders. As they got closer to the basket, Max opened up. No one was defending him. Nico dribbled hard toward the basket, but Jenna zoomed in front of him, blocking his path. Max waved his hands. "Nico! Nico!" he called. "Over here! I'm open!"

Nico glanced at Max but ignored him. Jenna continued to stand in his way. Nico dribbled the ball hard to the left, then to the right and, with seconds left, took a jump shot. His feet flew off the floor, and he held the ball high over his head. He pushed the bottom of it with his right hand, and the ball sailed toward the basket.

But Jenna jumped higher and shot her arms up. She wasn't able to block the shot, but the tops of her fingers brushed the basketball as it flew past. The ball tipped sideways and went past the hoop and out of bounds!

TWEET! Ms. Suraci's whistle blew. The first half was over.

Team Together

While Jenna's red team bounded off the court, the members of the MVP Club slunk back to the sidelines. Luke and Max plopped down on the bleachers and stared up at the ceiling. Kat and Alice grabbed their water bottles. Nico rolled a basketball from hand to hand and looked at the floor.

"We should be beating them!" Nico finally said. "We're a better team."

The rest of the MVP Club nodded but didn't say anything. Everyone was in a bad mood.

Then Jason stepped forward. "You *are* a better team," he said. "But the problem is you're not playing as a team."

"What do you mean?" Nico asked. "We're all out there. Of course we're a team!"

"No, you're not," Jason said. "You guys will lose if you keep playing like this. You're all playing separately. You have to pass the ball. You can't try to make every play all by yourself! You'll never win like that."

The MVP Club was quiet. Jason looked nervous, like maybe he had said the wrong thing.

Nico stepped forward. "Jason, you're right!" he said. "We're all grumpy because we've been competing against each other to win the sneakers."

Kat nodded. "I know we'd all like to win the sneakers," she said. "But let's forget about the popcorn competition and work together to beat Jenna's team. Anyway, to win the sneakers, our *team* has to sell the most popcorn, and we're really far behind."

"Maybe," Luke said. "But if we worked *together* to sell the popcorn, we'd have a much better chance of coming in first. Then we'd win the sweatshirts *and* one of us would win the sneakers!"

"But what do we do with the sneakers?" Max asked. "There's only one pair."

"We could share," Luke said. "I'd get them on Monday. Nico gets them on Tuesday, Alice gets them on Wednesday, you get them on Thursday, and Kat gets them on Friday. It's perfect!"

Kat laughed. "That's the dumbest thing I ever heard," she said. "My feet are smaller than your big clown feet! Plus, your feet stink like a skunk eating rotten eggs in a garbage bag! There's no way I'd want to wear the sneakers after you've been wearing them."

Nico held up his hand. "Hey, we can't do anything with the sneakers unless we win them," he said. "So let's work together to win, and then we'll figure out who gets to wear them!"

The rest of the MVP Club members nodded. "Good idea," Max said. "Maybe we can start after we *win!*"

"High five!" Nico called. They gathered in a circle. "Okay, Jason, what else should we be doing if we want to win this game?"

"Well, I have to go walk my dogs soon, but here's what I think," he said. Jason went over his notes from the first half of the game. He made a lot of suggestions on how Nico, Luke, Max, Alice, and Kat could work together better. They needed to think like a team. Jason suggested that they don't try to make any more three-pointers in the third quarter. Instead, he told them to keep passing and cutting to the hoop until someone is open. "The defense will get tired, and someone is bound to get open," he said.

TWEET! It was time for the second half!

Jason grabbed his backpack and headed out the door as the MVP Club hit the court. They played like a new team. Instead of hogging every ball, Luke and Nico kept passing it to anyone who was open. Within the first two minutes, the team had scored three times and stopped the red team twice in a row on defense!

The second half flew by. By the start of the fourth quarter, the MVP Club had made up a lot of lost ground. Jason's strategy had worked like a miracle. Whenever the clock stopped, the red team players put their hands on their knees, trying to catch their breath. The blue team was only six points behind. On the next possession, Jenna guarded Max tightly. At the three-point line, Max faked hard left and Jenna stumbled.

He drove to the basket and laid it in for the score!

The red team seemed rattled. Now they were playing like the MVP Club had been in the first half. Within two minutes they had fouled both Kat and Alice, who both made their free throws to score even more points!

But as the clock ticked down toward the end of the game, they were still behind. The red team was ahead by three points and they had the ball. It looked like they might even score again. But as they were running toward their basket, Kat caught a pass meant for Jenna!

Before the red team could recover and play defense, Kat spun around and ran downcourt. With no one defending the basket, she dribbled to the hoop and scored!

The blue team was down by one with just a minute left!

Jenna's team threw the ball in. Jenna passed it to Becky. As the red team closed in on the basket, the clock started to run out. They passed the ball around to waste more time.

Finally, Becky passed the ball back to Jenna, who zoomed in close to the basket for a shot. She planted her feet, set her shoulders, and tossed the ball.

But Luke jumped right in front of her! He sprang up high and swatted the ball!

Kat grabbed the ball before it could go out of bounds and tossed it to Luke, who was sprinting down the court. None of the red team players were near him! The clock inched toward zero. 5 . . . 4 . . . 3 . . . , it read.

"SHOOOOOOOOT!" yelled the fans in the bleachers. Luke dribbled one final time and pulled up to shoot the basketball. He was only a few feet past half-court.

With all of his might, Luke heaved the ball toward the basket. The ball arced slowly through the air. Every player stopped where they were and watched it fly.

WHUMP! The ball bounced off the backboard.

SWISH! It dropped through the net.

TWEET! Ms. Suraci's whistle blew. The game was over.

Luke had scored!

A Good Try

"Woo-hoo!" Kat said as her team bounded off the court. "We did it!"

The blue team had won!

Nico gave everyone high fives as they walked by. "Pack your bags because we're going to the Big City Basketball Blowout this weekend!"

Luke was the last in line. When he got to where Nico was standing, he stopped. He and Nico stared at each other for a moment. Then Nico held up both hands for a double high five. "Way to go, teammate!" he said. "Great job!"

Luke smiled and high-fived Nico. *SMAAAAACK!*

"Thanks, Nico," Luke said. "Jason was right! We should have been working together from the start."

They ran to join Alice, Kat, and Max on the bleachers. They were sipping from their water bottles and resting. Nico unzipped his backpack and dug around for a moment. Then he pulled out a big bag of snack mix.

"Hey, let's celebrate by trying my newest creation," Nico said. He liked to experiment in the kitchen. He was always coming up with new sports foods and snack mixes. "I call it my Rebound Recipe. It'll pick you up when you miss a shot!"

Luke raised his hand. "Is that really why it's called Rebound Recipe?" he asked. "Or is it because the snack mix will rebound on you when you eat it and it comes back up? Maybe we'd better wait until we're closer to the bathroom!"

"Luke!" Kat said. She swatted his shoulder. "That's disgusting!"

Alice dribbled a basketball as the

others munched on Nico's Rebound Recipe. "Hey, it's great we won the game," she said. "But now we need to find a way to win the popcorn sales competition."

"The first step would be to work together like we just did on the court," Max said. "Now that we won the game, I don't care which of us wins the sneakers, as long as one of us does!"

"Me neither," Nico said.

"Great!" Max said. "All in favor say 'Jump shot.'"

"JUMP SHOT!" said the group.

"Motion passed!" Max said. "The MVP Club is working together!"

Nico passed more of his snack mix around as the team brainstormed new ways to sell their popcorn.

"I'm not sure it's going to be any easier to sell it as a group," Kat said. "A lot of people I tried to sell to said they weren't very interested in plain old popcorn."

Nico nodded. "I heard that, too," he said. "But we can't give up!"

Luke popped another handful of Nico's Rebound Recipe in his mouth and started chewing. Then he stopped and looked in the bag of snack mix.

"Hey, Nico," he said after he swallowed. "What's in here?"

"Nuts, some cereal, a few bits of chocolate, some dried bananas, and a special mix of spices from my grandfather in Mexico," Nico said. "Chili powder, cocoa, cumin, garlic powder, and oregano, I think."

"Do you have more of the spice mix?" Luke asked.

"Sure," Nico said. "I have a bunch of it at home."

Luke hopped up from the bleachers. "I have an idea," he said. "What if we give away some of Nico's spice mix when we sell the popcorn? It would make the popcorn different, and more people might be interested in it."

"Great idea!" Alice said. Everyone else agreed. The team packed up their things and ran out to get their bikes.

As soon as they got to Nico's house, they started working. Max and Alice measured small amounts of spice mix into plastic snack bags that they got from Nico's mother. Each customer who bought a bag of popcorn would get a small package of spice mix with it. When they finished, the MVP Club headed out to sell popcorn. Since Nico had sold popcorn on his street yesterday, they started a couple of streets over. Max and Alice took one side of the street, and Nico, Luke, and Kat took the other. They spent the next twenty minutes going from door to door.

But even with the spice mix, the popcorn wasn't selling much better than the day before. After ringing doorbells on half the block, the MVP Club had sold just five bags of popcorn! They took a break near a tree.

"I thought this would work," Nico said. "It's a great idea."

Luke took a bow and pointed to his head. "It *is* a great idea," he said. "Especially because I thought of it! And I just had another idea, but you can't laugh."

Everyone looked at Luke. "What?" Nico asked.

"Well, I learned that giving out samples at the movie theater wasn't a great sales move," Luke said. "But maybe it would work with the spice mix. Let's mix up a few sample bags of spicy popcorn and hand out samples when we ring the doorbells. When people taste the spicy popcorn, I bet they'll buy some!"

Alice shrugged. "We don't have much to lose," she said. "We can try it with just a couple bags." She opened the top of two popcorn bags and dumped a spice mix packet in each. After closing the tops and shaking the bags, everyone took a kernel.

"Mmm . . . that's good," Kat said. "Let's go!"

The MVP Club split up again and started going door to door, handing out free samples of spicy popcorn.

A few minutes later, Nico ran down the front steps of the house they had stopped at. "It worked! It worked!" he yelled to Max and Alice. "We sold three bags at the first house!"

"I know!" Alice called. "We sold two!"

By the time the MVP Club had finished ringing all the doorbells on the street, they were out of popcorn! Everyone ran back to Nico's house to add up their sales.

They pooled their money into a pile in the middle of the kitchen table and counted it. "I can't believe how many bags of popcorn we sold!" Max said. "We have to be in the lead now!"

"Let's see," Kat said. She took her phone out of her pocket. "I took a picture of the popcorn sales poster before we left school." Kat was always taking pictures.

She swiped at her phone with her finger and gave it a couple of taps. The picture of the popcorn sales poster came up. She stared at it for a moment and her shoulders slumped. Then she turned the phone and held it up for the others to see.

"Oh," Alice said.

"That can't be!" Nico said.

"It is," Kat said.

Even with all the sales they had just made, the MVP Club was still behind the purple team *and* Jenna's red team!

A New Plan

"Come on! We've got all afternoon to beat Jenna's team," Nico said. "If we could beat them on the basketball court, we can beat them in the popcorn sale."

It was Thursday afternoon, and school had just let out for the day. That morning, the MVP Club had given their updated sales numbers to Ms. Suraci. Kat's photo was correct. It was going to be hard to catch up. But Nico was determined to try.

When they arrived at Ms. Suraci's office, the MVP Club had to wait for the purple team to get its new bags of popcorn.

"Come on in!" Ms. Suraci waved the MVP Club into her office. She pointed to a small pile of bags in the corner. "Help yourself. You're the last team to stop by, so it's all yours!"

Nico walked over to the pile. "But there are only ten bags of popcorn here," he said. "We need a lot more if we're going to catch up to Jenna's team!"

Ms. Suraci sighed. "Sorry, Nico, but that's all I have," she said. "Some of the teams sold so much popcorn earlier in the week that I had to limit today's refills to ten per team."

"Isn't there any way to get more?" Alice asked.

Ms. Suraci shook her head. "The sales drive is over tomorrow, and there isn't any time for the school to get more. Sorry," she said.

Nico tried to make the best of it. "Okay, thanks," he said. "Come on, team, let's at least go out and sell these."

Nico scooped up the remaining bags, and the MVP Club headed out to make some sales. Instead of going back to Nico's house, they decided to try one of the side streets near the school. They mixed one bag with Nico's spice mix to make samples. It only took them about fifteen minutes to sell the other nine bags with packets of spice mix. When they were done, they walked back to school.

"Now what?" Luke asked as he hung upside down on bars at the playground. "Do we wait around to clap when Jenna and her team turn in their money for their final sales? There's no way we can win."

"I know," Max said. "Our popcorn was selling so well with Nico's spice mix. We would have had a good chance to win if Ms. Suraci hadn't run out of popcorn."

"We ran out of cereal at my house last week," Alice said. "But it wasn't a problem because my mother just went down to the store to get some more."

"What?" Luke asked. He was still swinging upside down.

"I said my mother just ran to the store when we were out of cereal last week," Alice said.

BAM!

Luke clapped his hands together and dropped to the ground. Then he stood up and faced the MVP Club.

"That's it!" he said. "We just need to get more popcorn!"

Alice looked at Nico and the others. "Uh, hello, Luke? We just tried that," she said. "Remember? Ms. Suraci is out."

Luke smiled. "I know," he said. "But that doesn't mean we can't get it from somewhere else! Just because Ms. Suraci is out of popcorn doesn't mean *we* have to be out of popcorn! What if we go to the store? We can cook up more popcorn, and then add Nico's spice right to it! We'll get some bags and sell it door to door, just like we were doing before."

Everyone was quiet for a moment. Then Nico did a backward handspring!

"I love it!" Nico said as he landed on his feet. "But I think we should check with Ms. Suraci first to make sure it's okay. Wait here."

Nico sprinted inside the school. A few minutes later, he burst out the front door and gave the group a thumbs-up.

"We're good!" he called out. "Ms. Suraci said it was fine with her if we made our own popcorn to sell. We just have to put it in the same size bags."

"Oh yeah!" Luke said. "We're in the popcorn business!"

The MVP Club hopped on their bikes and pedaled to the grocery store on Main Street. They pooled their money and bought a big bag of popcorn kernels. Then they headed to Nico's house, where Alice organized them into teams. Nico and Luke were in charge of cooking the popcorn and making the spice mix. Kat was in charge of bagging the popcorn. Max and Alice would sell it. To make things easier, they decided to mix the spices right with the popcorn, since it was selling so well.

As soon as the first batch of popcorn was finished and bagged, Alice and Max went out to sell it. No one answered the door at the first house. At the next four houses, they sold a total of sixteen bags of popcorn. At the fifth house, a dog started barking crazily in the background when they rang the doorbell.

A few moments later, a white-haired woman who looked like a grandmother answered. Behind her, a medium-size, curly-haired black dog pushed its nose up to the glass of the door.

The grandmother looked at Alice and Max and then nodded at the dog. "That's just Lucy," she said. "Don't pay any attention to her. She doesn't have much of a chance to get out because it's hard for me to walk her. She gets excited anytime the doorbell rings."

Alice immediately crouched down and smiled at the door. The dog jumped up and licked the glass.

"What a nice dog!" Alice said as she stood up. "I'm Alice, and this is my friend Max. We're raising money for our basketball team at school by selling bags of popcorn. They also include a special spice mix that we made. Would you like to try some?"

"Sure," the grandmother said. She opened the door and came out to the porch with her dog. "My name's Emily."

Max gave Emily a sample of popcorn as Alice knelt back down to pet the dog. Lucy climbed up into Alice's lap and licked her cheeks as Emily went into the house to get some money. When she came back, she bought four bags of popcorn. She was just about to close the door when Alice spoke up.

"Lucy is so sweet!" Alice said. "We have a friend named Jason who has a dog-walking service. I'm sure he'd be happy to walk Lucy if you wanted."

Emily gave Alice a big smile. "That would be wonderful!" she said. "If you give me his number, I can call him."

"Sure," Alice said. She wrote down Jason's number on one of Emily's notepads, and then she and Max headed to the next house.

But as they walked away, Alice grabbed Max's arm. "Come on," Alice said. "I've got an idea."

They rushed back to Nico's house. As soon as they arrived, Alice logged on to Nico's computer. A few minutes later, she printed out a piece of paper and handed it to Max. The MVP Club read it. The page had a picture of a big shaggy dog on it. Underneath the dog was a phone number and some words:

"Since we're going door to door to sell our popcorn, I thought we could also pass out flyers for Jason's dog-walking service," Alice said.

"That's a great idea!" Nico said. "It's the least we can do after he helped us win the basketball game!"

Alice printed more flyers while Max restocked with more bags of spicy popcorn. Then he and Alice headed out to sell. At each house they went to that had a dog, they also passed out a flyer.

The MVP Club worked all afternoon. Luke and Nico continued to make more batches of spicy popcorn. Kat bagged everything. And Max and Alice kept running to Nico's to get more popcorn and then rushing out to sell it.

Before everyone left to go home for dinner, Alice gathered them around Nico's kitchen table.

"Well, we tried," Alice said. "I don't know if we're going to win, but we gave it our best shot!"

Then she leaned over and dumped a huge pile of money in the middle of the table!

A First-Place Finish

"I can't wait to see the numbers on the popcorn sales poster!" Alice said. The members of the MVP Club had just parked their bikes outside school and were headed for the front steps.

"I know," Nico said. "With all the popcorn we made and sold, we have to be close to winning!"

But when they made it inside the school, the wall where the poster had been was bare.

"Where is the poster?" Luke asked Caleb, one of the kids from the purple team, who was standing nearby.

Caleb shook his head. "Ms. Suraci took it down last night. Everyone's supposed to stop by her office and tell her their final sales. She's having a meeting after school in the gym to tell us the winners."

Luke sighed loudly. "You mean we have to wait all day to find out who won?" he asked. "Making it through a school day is tough enough, but this is going to be impossible!"

Kat tugged on Luke's shoulder. "Come on," she said. "You can do it. I guess you're just popped out from making all that popcorn yesterday!"

Luke rolled his eyes. "That's awful," he said. "Popped out? Is that the best you could do, sis?"

"I'll turn in our money and tell Ms. Suraci our totals. I think we should give Nico most of the sales since his spice mix saved us," Alice said.

"Good idea," Max agreed, and the rest of the team nodded.

"Okay, see you in class!" Alice said.

Even though it was like any other day at school, it seemed like the clock would never make it to the afternoon.

But the last bell of the day finally rang, and all the basketball teams ran to the gym. They gathered on the bleachers. When Jason walked into the gym, the MVP Club waved him over to sit with them.

Ms. Suraci stood under the basketball net. On a card table next to her were five green T-shirts, five green sweatshirts, and the pair of sneakers.

TWEET!

Ms. Suraci blew her whistle and held up her hand. "Okay, I know this is exciting, but let's be quiet so we can find out who won!" she said.

The kids on the bleachers settled down, and the gym became very quiet.

"I want to thank everyone for working so hard on the fund-raiser," Ms. Suraci said. "We raised more money this year than we've ever raised in the past!"

Ms. Suraci clapped. Everyone joined in. When the clapping stopped, Ms. Suraci continued. "Everyone did such a great job selling popcorn. But the winner of the second-place prize is the PURPLE TEAM!"

"Yahoo!" yelled Tommy, the purple team captain. He and the other members of his team ran up to Ms. Suraci to collect their prizes. They all slipped on the special T-shirts and held their hands up high.

Tommy stepped in front of Ms. Suraci and pretended to give an awards speech. "I'd like to thank my parents, and my teachers, and all the little people who helped me reach this great achievement," he said into a pretend microphone. "I'll never forget you. I also want to thank my nursery school teacher, my barber, the guy at the shoe store, and the person I passed on the street today."

Tommy was about to thank even more people, but one of his teammates pulled him back to the bleachers.

Ms. Suraci shook her head. "Whew! That seemed like it could have gone on for a while," she said.

She held up one of the green sweat-shirts that read *FRANKLIN BASKETBALL*.

"And now for the winner of the first-place team prize," she said. "Even though this team didn't start out selling a lot of popcorn, they finished strong.

According to my numbers, the winning team sold forty-four more bags than the purple team. First place in our popcorn sales competition goes to the BLUE TEAM!"

Max, Alice, Nico, Kat, and Luke jumped off the bleachers.

"I can't believe it!" Kat said. "We did it!"

The MVP Club high-fived each other and ran to get their shirts. Alice reached Ms. Suraci first. She pulled the green sweatshirt over her head and flashed a big smile. Luke struggled to get his on.

Ms. Suraci held up her hands for quiet. "Settle down! We have one last prize to give out," she said, "to the person on the blue team who sold the most bags of popcorn."

Luke and Nico glanced at each other. Then they smiled and exchanged a high five.

Ms. Suraci picked up the sneakers from the table and held them over her head.

"And the grand prize winner of the sneakers is . . . ," she said with a pause.

The kids could hear the clock on the wall ticking.

The Real Winner

"Nico!" Ms. Suraci called out. "Come and get your sneakers! See me after if you need a different size."

"Wowee!" Nico said as he picked up the sneakers and held them over his head. Everyone clapped for him.

"That's it for today," Ms. Suraci said. "Thanks to your hard work, we have enough money for every team to go to a travel tournament this year!"

The kids clapped and stamped their feet on the bleachers until Ms. Suraci ended the meeting and told everyone to go home. The MVP Club was supposed to show up at the gym the next morning at eight o'clock to go to the Big City Basketball Blowout.

As the other teams left the gym, the MVP Club and Jason crowded around Nico's new sneakers to examine them.

"Wow! These are so cool!" Jason said. "They're so light. You'll be able to run really fast in them."

"And I love the silver stripe on the side," Kat said. She pointed to a sparkly line that ran down each side of the sneakers. It glittered in the light.

Nico handed the shoes to Luke. "Well, what do you want to do with the shoes?" he asked. "How about you take the left one, and I take the right one?"

Luke laughed. "We could do that," he said. "But I've got a better idea. Come over here for a minute." Luke pulled Nico away from the group. They huddled near the bleachers and whispered to each other. Then they walked back to the group.

"What's your big idea?" Max asked Luke. "Have you decided to take turns wearing them?"

"No," said Luke. "Nico and I came

up with a better idea. We never would have won the sneakers if we hadn't been working together as a team. And Jason is the one who helped us learn that during the basketball game. Without Jason, we wouldn't have won the basketball game. And Nico wouldn't have won the sneakers."

The other members of the MVP Club nodded. Max and Nico high-fived with Jason.

"That's why Nico and I have decided to give our sneakers to Jason!" Luke continued.

Jason turned to Luke. Jason's eyes were wide, and he had a big smile on his face. Luke handed Jason the sneakers. Jason looked from Luke to Nico and back.

"Really? You're going to give these to me?" he asked. "*Thanks!* That's so cool. I've never had sneakers this nice!"

Jason kicked off his broken sneakers and pulled on the new ones. "They're the perfect size," he said. The sneakers looked great on Jason's feet. He ran a circle around the group. "These are awesome!" he said. "They're so fast. Now I'll be able to walk dogs twice as quickly as before!" He beamed from ear to ear.

"Speaking of dogs, how did our flyers work?" Alice asked. "We sure passed out a lot of them."

Jason slid to a halt. "They worked really well!" he said. "That was such a good idea you came up with, Alice. I got five new customers and three more I'm going to meet with later this week. The extra money will help at home. My mom and I appreciate it. We're saving money to move to an apartment."

"I'm so glad," Alice said.

Jason checked the time. "Thanks for everything," he said. He pointed to the new sneakers on his feet. "I'd love to stay, but *these* dogs have to walk *those* new dogs you got for me with the flyers! Good luck in your tournament tomorrow!"

Jason picked up his backpack and ran out of the gym.

"Now what?" Alice asked.

"Well, I'm sure Nico wants to get some practice shots in before tomorrow's game," Luke said. "He would never let an empty gym go to waste!"

"I hadn't thought of it, but thanks for the idea, Luke!" Nico said. "Let's play a quick scrimmage game before we leave."

Luke rolled his eyes. "But we need to rest before the big game."

Nico picked up a basketball. "Not if we want to win!" he said.

"Wait!" Kat said. "I almost forgot. We have one other thing we have to do."

Kat and Alice walked over to the bleachers. Kat fished around in her backpack and pulled something out, but she kept it hidden from the rest of the MVP Club. She walked back to the group.

"Luke! We've all agreed that if you don't want to practice today, you can take the day off," Alice said. "Not only did you make the winning basket in the game on Wednesday, but you're the one who came up with the idea to add Nico's spice mix to the popcorn. We never would have been able to win those sneakers and give them to Jason without your brilliant idea."

Kat took a step forward. "That's why we decided to award you the first ever basketball MVP award!"

Kat pulled her hands from behind her back and slipped an MVP medal around Luke's neck. The medal was a big picture of an orange basketball with a ribbon through it.

Luke examined the medal for a moment. "Thanks, everyone!" he said with a big smile. "But who said anything about taking the day off? If I won the basketball MVP medal, it must mean that I'm the best! So there's no way that I would pass up a chance to beat Nico."

Luke took the basketball from Nico's hands. "You know, I kinda let you win those sneakers," he said. "But I'm not going to let you win today."

Luke bumped Nico in the chest with the basketball. "Show me what you got," he said. "Game on!"

Basketball

BASKETBALL TEAMS. Basketball teams have five people playing at once.

MEASUREMENTS. A basketball hoop is eighteen inches wide. The hoop is mounted ten feet above the court on a backboard.

FREE THROWS. Free throws are when a player stands at the free throw line, also known as the foul line, and shoots the basketball at the hoop. A player gets free throws if an opponent fouls him. A foul is when a player breaks a rule or interferes with another player.

DRIBBLING. In basketball, dribbling isn't leaking water down your chin when drinking. Instead, dribbling is when a player bounces the basketball against the court while walking or running. But once a player stops dribbling, she has to either pass the ball or take a shot. Otherwise it's called a carry or double dribble.

PASS. Passing the ball is important in a basketball game. Players throw the ball to other players if they want to quickly move the ball around the court or if one player has a good shot.

DON'T TRAVEL! When you're playing basketball, you have to pay attention to your feet. You will be called for traveling if you move the wrong foot or take two or more steps without dribbling.

POSITIONS, PLEASE. The usual positions on a basketball team are guards, forwards, and centers. *Point guards* are experts at passing and moving the ball around. *Shooting guards* are good at taking shots and making baskets. *Small forwards* are good at just about everything, while *power forwards* are great at scoring. *Centers* usually play near the basket and may be the tallest players on the team. They are great at blocking and rebounding.

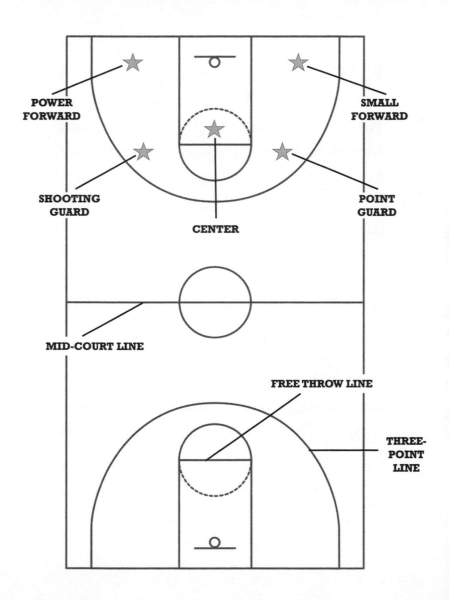

POWER
FORWARD

SMALL
FORWARD

SHOOTING
GUARD

POINT
GUARD

CENTER

MID-COURT LINE

FREE THROW LINE

THREE-
POINT
LINE

PEACH BASKETS. Basketball was invented in 1891 by Dr. James Naismith. He worked at the YMCA in Springfield, Massachusetts. He was trying to keep boys busy on a rainy day. To do that, he nailed a peach basket onto a ten-foot pole and had kids take shots at it. At first, they left the bottom on the basket. But they soon realized it was easier to cut a hole in the bottom, and basketball was born.

THE NBA. The National Basketball Association (NBA) is the top basketball league. There are currently thirty NBA teams. NBA teams typically play eighty or more games per year. Their championship is called the NBA Finals.

GREAT WORDS. Basketball has lots of fun words:

AIR BALL: A shot that misses the hoop and backboard completely.

ALLEY-OOP: When a player throws the ball to another player who jumps, catches the ball in midair, and pops it through the hoop.

FAST BREAK: When a team tries to move the ball up the court really fast to make a basket.

PUMP FAKE: Pretending to pass the ball.

REBOUND: Catching the ball when it bounces off the backboard.

SLAM DUNK: When a player jumps up and slams the ball down into the hoop with one or two hands.

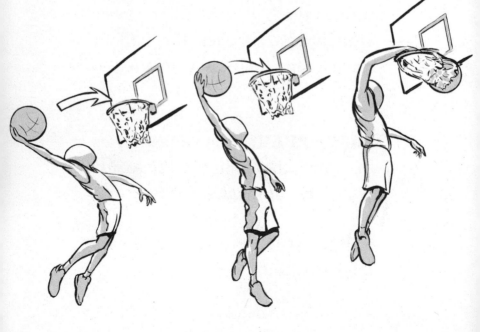

READY FOR MORE
SPORTS?

Check out the World Series in the first
Ballpark Mysteries Super Special!

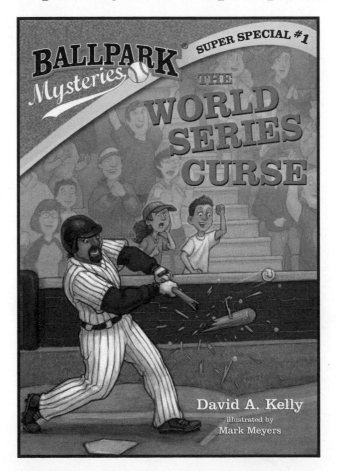

"What's a goat doing at Fenway Park?" Kate asked. She scratched the top of the goat's head gently.

"You've never heard of the Billy Goat Curse?" Louie asked. "It's followed us to Fenway. The guys on the Cubs think we might lose the World Series because of it!"

Mike and Kate shook their heads.

"I've heard about the Curse of the Bambino," Mike said. "That's when the Red Sox were cursed because they sold Babe Ruth to the Yankees."

"That's a different one," Louie said. "Ms. Sanders can tell you about the Billy Goat Curse. She's the owner of the Billy Goat Diner in Chicago."

The woman in the yellow shirt stood up. She shook hands with Mike and Kate. "I'm Sandra Sanders," she said. "A long time ago, the Cubs kicked my grandfather out of Wrigley Field because he brought his pet goat to the game. They said it smelled. My grandfather was angry that the Cubs made him leave, so he put a curse on the Cubs. He said the Cubs would never win another World Series because they weren't nice to his goat!"

Mike leaned over near the goat. He sniffed a few times. "Smells okay to me," he said. "But what's your goat doing here in Boston?"

"Well, my grandfather died a long time ago, so the Cubs are trying to lift the curse by being nice to me and my goat, Billy," Ms. Sanders said. "They've asked us to come to all the Cubs games this year. They hope that Billy will help break the curse so the Cubs will win the World Series!"

Mike looked at Big D. "But aren't the Red Sox worried they'll lose if the Cubs break the curse?" he asked.

Big D waved his hand and laughed. "We don't care about a goat," he said. "Louie and his Cubs could bring a whole farm with them if they wanted. I don't think it's going to help them win the series this year."

"Well, we need all the good luck we can get," Louie said. He reached over to pet the goat.

Ms. Sanders handed Mike and Kate a business card for the goat. It read:

LET THE BILLY GOAT IN
AND LET THE CURSE GO!
THIS YEAR OR NEXT, IT'S THE CUBS!

The back of the card listed all the billy goat stuff Ms. Sanders sold, including Billy Goat Club memberships. It also gave the goat's website, where fans could send comments or ask for funny advice from the goat.

"Fans sure love the goat, even if they don't like the curse," Ms. Sanders said. "Billy and I keep really busy selling Billy Goat Curse hats, T-shirts, and more. If we're lucky, someday the curse will be broken. But hopefully not before Billy retires!" Ms. Sanders gave a short laugh that was interrupted by a man running down the hallway.

He was an older man in a blue dress shirt and a polka-dot bow tie. The man stopped right in front of the goat.

"Red, what happened?" Ms. Sanders asked the man. "You were supposed to be watching Billy while I was at lunch!"

Red brushed his hair back. "I was," he said. "I checked on Billy a few minutes ago, and he was tied up just where you left him. There was a man in a blue jacket talking on a phone near him,

but everything was okay until I came back just now. Billy must have chewed through the rope."

"Well, Kate here caught him, so we're all set," Ms. Sanders said.

Louie slapped Red on the back. "Hi, Red! Good to see you," he said. "Mike and Kate, this is my good friend Red Remy. He's one of the most famous sports reporters in Chicago. Unfortunately, he's a big fan of Chicago's *other* major-league team, the Chicago White Sox. But at least he's not a fan of the Boston Red Sox!"

Red blushed and straightened his bow tie. He dropped his black messenger bag to the ground. "Well, the White Sox are my favorite team. But if they don't make the World Series, I guess the Cubs are the next best thing," he said. "But I hope next year it will be the White Sox!"

While they were talking, Mike examined the goat's rope. "Hey, this rope has a nice clean end. Someone must have untied him or cut the rope," he said.

Red laughed lightly. "Hmmm, it could have been that man in the blue jacket. I didn't think anything of it at the time, but he *was* near the goat."

Mike's eyes lit up. "What did he look like?" he asked. "Can you describe him?"

Red thought for a moment. "He was about my height. He had sandy brown hair. He was wearing tan pants and a blue jacket," he said. "And something about him looked a little shifty."

Kate leaned in to look at the rope while Red was answering Mike. Then she noticed the collar around the goat's neck. There was a luggage tag attached to it. Inside was a gray piece of paper with

writing on it. The words were printed in block letters in thin blue ink.

"Um, Louie," she said. "I think this is for you." She pulled the luggage tag off the goat.

"Why, what does it say?" Louie asked.

Kate read the note.

THE BILLY GOAT CURSE STRIKES AGAIN!
Your Good Luck Goat Has Left the Building.
The Cubs Will Lose the World Series!

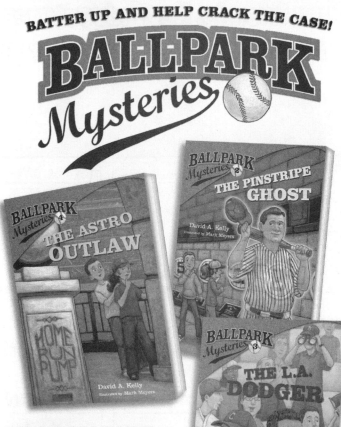